CIRCLE DOGS

by Kevin Henkes illustrated by Dan Yaccarino
Greenwillow Books, New York

Gouache paints were used to prepare the full-color art. The text type is Futura Condensed. Text copyright © 1998 by Kevin Henkes. Illustrations copyright © 1998 by Dan Yaccarino. All rights reserved. No part of this book may be reproduced or utilized in any form or by any means, electronic or mechanical, including photocopying, recording, or by any information storage and retrieval system, without permission in writing from the Publisher, Greenwillow Books, an imprint of HarperCollins Publishers, 10 East 53rd Street, New York, NY 10022. www.harperchildrens.com   Manufactured in China. South China Printing Company Ltd.   First Edition   12 13 SCP 10 9 8 7 6 5

Library of Congress Cataloging-in-Publication Data:
Circle dogs / by Kevin Henkes ; pictures by Dan Yaccarino.   p.   cm.
Summary: Circle dogs live in a square house with a square yard, eat circle snacks, and dig circle holes.
ISBN 0-688-15446-8 (trade). ISBN 0-688-15447-6 (lib. bdg.) ISBN 0-06-443757-4 (pbk.) [1. Dogs—Fiction. 2. Shape—Fiction]
I. Yaccarino, Don, ill.   II. Title.   PZ7.H389Ck   1998   [E]—dc21   97-33037   CIP   AC

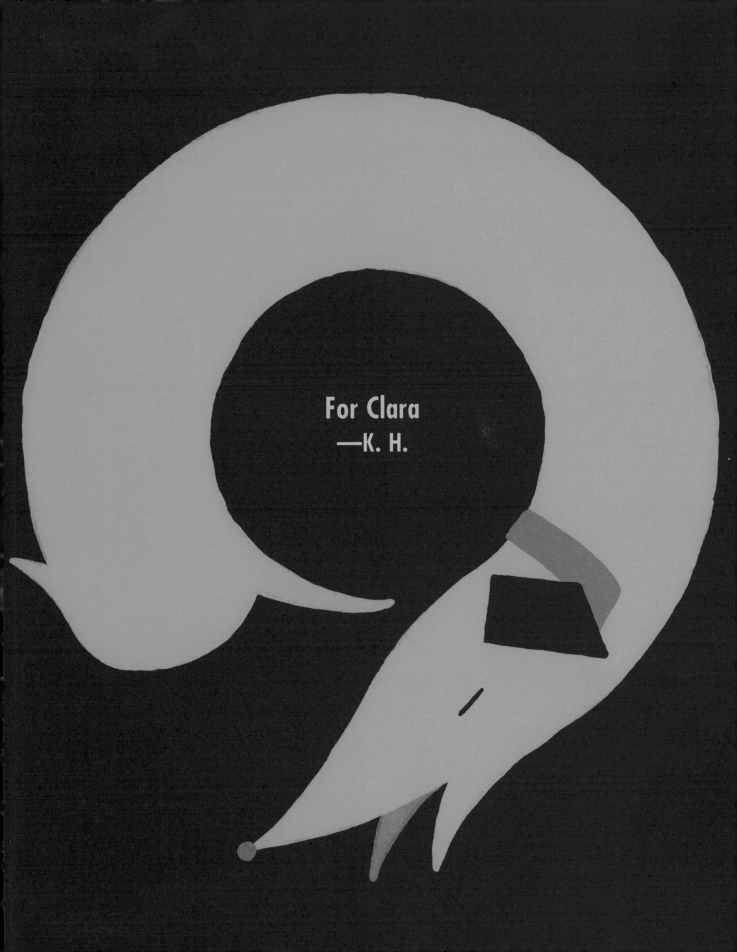

For Clara
—K. H.

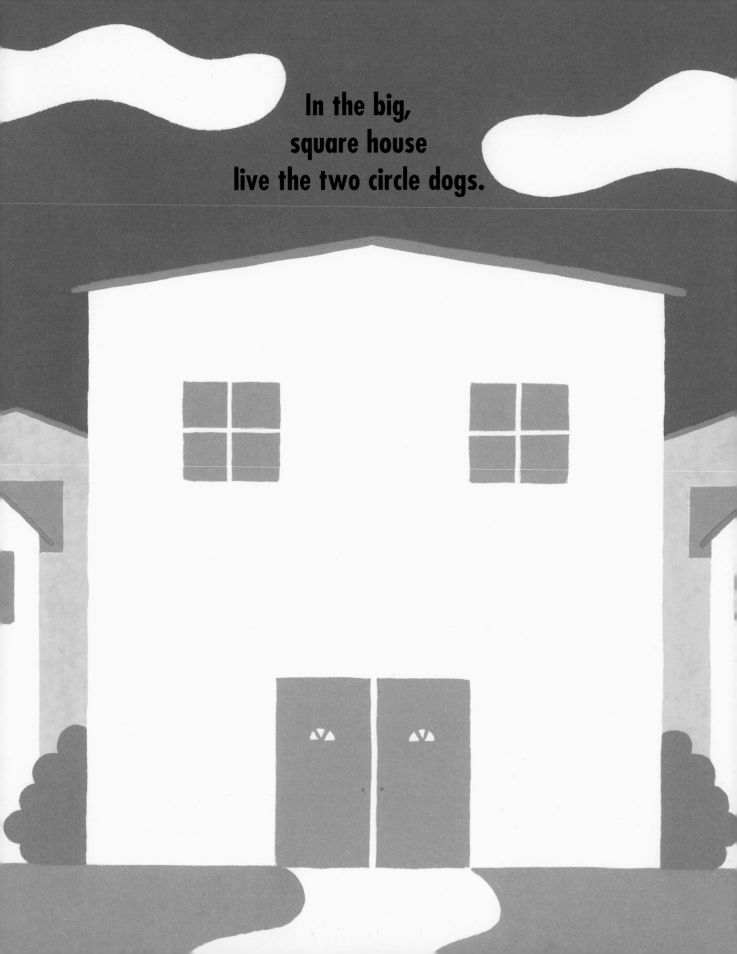

In the big,
square house
live the two circle dogs.

See the dogs?
See the circles?
Shhh. They're sleeping now.

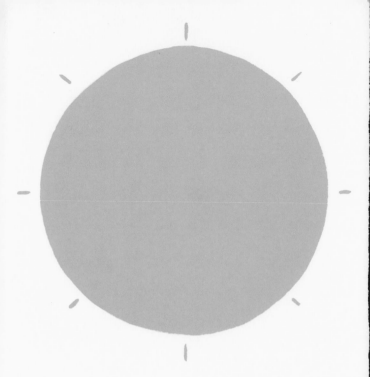

But when the sun comes up

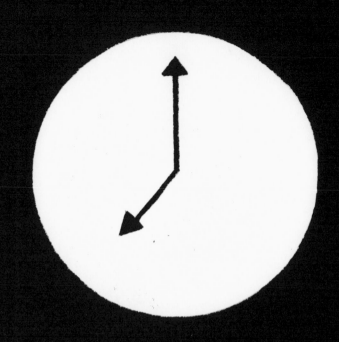

and the alarm goes off

and the baby cries

and the birds chatter—

the circle dogs wake up.

Clink-clank, clink-clank, clink-clank, clink.
Hear their tags?
Mrooon, mro-o-o-o-on.
They stretch and stretch and moan and yawn.

Flip-flap,

flip-flap.

Swish, swoosh,

swish.

Their tails wave.

**Get up! Get up!
Play with us. Now!**

After good-morning kisses for everyone,

Papa lets them out to run.

Run, run, run in the big, square yard.

Circle dogs snap at the air.

Maybe there's invisible food in the sky.

Now circle dogs have triangle ears.
Look, they stand up like toy soldiers.

**Are those Baby's pink socks hanging out of their mouths?
No, silly! Those are tongues.**

When circle dogs dig circle holes,
Mama and Papa yell, "No, no, no!"

Now they're back inside the house.
Look out!
Baby's face smells milky.
Sniff, sniff, sniff.

Big Sister's kind of messy.
Lick, lick, lick.

Papa drops his toast.
Oops! Where did it go?
The circle dogs know.

Mama fills their circle bowls.
Kibble-clatter, kibble-nibble.
Gulp, smack, gone!

Now they sleep

and sleep

and sleep

and sleep.

**One leg twitches, then another.
Maybe they're dreaming.**

Now they sleep

and sleep

and sleep some more.

Maybe they see doughnuts and moons and bones as big as cats.

Do they ever wake up?
You bet!
Just wait for the doorbell to ring.
Bring-ding, bring-ding,
bring-ding-dong.

Wooof, wooof, wooof.

Or for the mail to arrive.
Stomp, stomp,
whoosh, whoosh,
bam, stomp, stomp.
Grrrrr, grrrrr, grrrrr.

Or for friends to stop by.
Knock, knock, knock.
Come out! Come out!
Arf, aarf, aaarf.

They run.

They jump.

They bounce like balls.

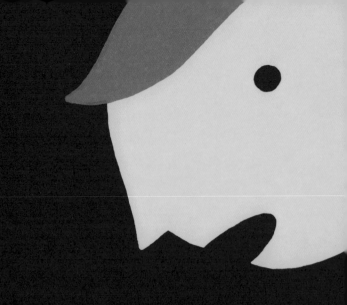

Mama calls them pooches.   Papa calls them hounds.

"Those pooches!" says Mama.   "Those hounds!" says Papa.

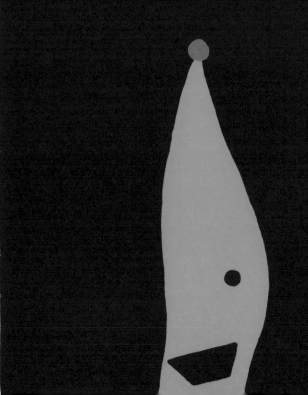

"I'm a dog!" says Big Sister.

Baby is too,
with a sloppy kiss for everyone.

Circle dogs like circle snacks—
crunch, crunch, crunch—
right from your hand.

They like to play.
They like to roll.
They like to eat.

And then they like to sleep and sleep and sleep and sleep.

In the big, square house
live the two circle dogs.

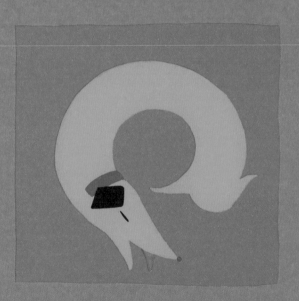

See the dogs?
See the circles?